SCARLET IN GASLIGHT

is based on the Dracula characters created by Bram Stoker and the Sherlock Holmes characters created by Sir Arthur Conan Doyle.

The Sherlock Holmes characters appear by arrangement with Dame Jean Conan Doyle.

Martin Powell and **Wayne R. Smith**: Plot

Martin Powell: Script

Seppo Makinen: Artist

Pat Brosseau: Letterer

Seppo Makinen: Cover Illustration

Bruce Timm: Cover Coloring

Publisher
Dave Olbrich

Editor-In-Chief
Chris Ulm

Creative Director
Tom Mason

SCARLET IN GASLIGHT
Malibu Graphics, Inc.
1355 Lawrence Drive #212
Newbury Park, CA 91320
805/499-3015

Scott Rosenberg/President. Chris Ulm/Vice-President.
Tom Mason/Secretary. Dave Olbrich/Treasurer.
Christine Hsu/Controller.

Second Printing: May 1990

$9.95/$11.95 in Canada
ISBN #0-944735-09-6

INTRODUCTION

I first met Kentucky born Martin Powell about three years ago when he wrote to me via an amateur cartoon organization we were once affiliated with. I found his letter to be charming, hip, and a tad macabre.

Soon after, I spoke to him over the phone and found my initial perceptions true, but intentionally subtle. Later, I learned that Martin had mastered this subtlety to terrorize the eyes through sequential whispers of horror. Martin proposed that we work on a comic book together, and I immediately accepted. Thus, *The Verdict*, was born. Then one day, he told me he was writing a mini-series titled: *Scarlet In Gaslight* "borrowing characters created by Sir Arthur Conan Doyle, and Bram Stoker."

I did not know of these authors until I was informed of their popular creations: Sherlock Holmes, and Dracula, respectively. Two legends I never really had much knowledge of nor interest in, but certainly had seen them through Hollywood endeavors. I expressed that it was a good idea for marketing reasons, but did not think he could be exceptionally original with established heroes. Well...three months later, Martin sent me *Scarlet In Gaslight* #1, and startled me. For a short space of time, I had become 100% *wrong!*

The comic knocked my socks off! The traditional, classical world of Holmes, and Dracula, had been perverted with. I think the reason why Martin, asked me to write the introduction to this four-issue compilation, is because I was a virgin fan, with only popular peripheral understanding of the notorious cast. I witnessed as Martin twisted legends into breathing people, and was introduced to Powell's revolutionary vision of thes myths personal plights and desires.

Sherlock Holmes is the phenomenal detective with hints of an on-and-off history of sexual trauma, and drug abuse, displays his only secure foundation, by solving the impossible. Count Dracula, Lord of the Vampires, is a lost romantic who fights a 500 year-old war with eternal Hell while marked with the curse of having to steal the precious fluid of crimson life. Professor Moriarty, Holmes' evil nemesis, who cares not of life, nor honor, but of vengeance, and hate. Dr. John Watson, the integral partner of Holmes, who seems to be the only sane one to accept the illogical, and irrational. Dr. Van Helsing, an old man, with enough faith, obsession, and fear, to crawl with his garlic and silver, to the very end. Last but not least, Mycroft Holmes, Sherlock's genius older brother, plays an intriguing cameo appearance that begs for more attention.

Martin hooked me line and sinker from beginning to end and made a wise decision by choosing Seppo Makinen's, delicate, renaissance line. Makinen's work puts the atmosphere in proper expressionistic hues and patchwork plaids. Seppo's renditions of the famous band are executed with jealous ease. Please waste no more time. Read and behold.

Dean E. Haspiel
New York City
June, 1988

FOREWORD

"Ave Sherlock Morituri Et Cetera."

That is to say: Hail, Sherlock, we who shall one day pass and be forgotten, salute you, undying, who some say never lived!

A charming sentiment, written by Sherlockian scholar Vincent Starrett in 1933 and, over a half century later, still essentially true. Sherlock Holmes is as popular today as during the original run of his series of tales beginning in 1887 as written by Sir Arthur Conan Doyle. Indeed, the Holmes legend has recently enjoyed a kind of renaissance since last year's centennial celebration, including, by a happy coincidence, this past November's publication of *Scarlet In Gaslight*, which marked a span of one hundred years—almost to the day—of the Detective's first appearance in print.

One of the most gratifying of the letters from readers of the mini-series wanted to thank me for "bringing Sherlock Holmes back to life." A flattering comment to be sure, though hardly a true one. Holmes hasn't risen from the dead, nor has he ever needed to. From the start the character has managed to retain his famous profile in a variety of novels, short stories, stage plays, games, operas, ballets, films and television programs.

To my knowledge the original sixty stories have never been out of print, and various editions must number in the hundreds of millions translated into practically every spoken language on the planet. As a result, Holmes—as a popular character—is one of the most widely recognized fictional creations of all time, making his creator one of the world's most read authors.

Strangely, Sherlock Holmes has taken on a life seemingly independent from his origins; I believe it is safe to say that there are surely millions who know the name of the Detective and yet have never heard of hansom cabs, gaslight, Queen Victoria, or even Sir Arthur Conan Doyle.

Still, with all this fame and popularity on his side, The Great Detective has seldom enjoyed his own successful comic series. An exception to this rule was the long-running newspaper strip by Edith Meiser/Frank Giacoia which ran in the 1950s (and which Eternity is reprinting for the first time complete and uncut), and Renegade's *Cases Of Sherlock Holmes*, reworkings of the authentic tales strikingly illustrated by artist Dan Day.

Still, nothing could have prepared me for the success of *Scarlet In Gaslight* as each issue, to my surprise and delight, continued to sell out, often within two weeks of publication. As much as a writer is tempted, in all justice, I don't feel the credit points directly to me or to Seppo; obviously the comics-reading public *wants* Sherlock Holmes.

In preparing to write *Scarlet* I realized that most comics readers would find transcribed panels from the Conan Doyle stories dry and flat on the illustrated page, but I admit that I was merely guessing when I added the fantasy element to Holmes, feeling that I was hopefully anticipating a waiting audience. Holmes' almost purely mental action and smug certainty can seem dated and stilted to the modern reader, paticularly the new discoverer.

What was needed, I felt, was a new approach to the character, a different kind of adventure that would reflect a new light on the Holmes mythos—an alien experience for the Detective outside his well-ordered and logical world.

I decided to concentrate on presenting a fresh vision of Holmes—without departing from Conan Doyle—creating a deeper portrait of his personality, exposing the taboos of the Detective's early life and developing a disturbing twist to his long battle with Professor Moriarty. Count Dracula, another favorite of mine, is really a guest star in this tale.

As drawn by Seppo I had to be extremely careful as to how much I involved The Count in the story, as his physical appearance causes him to clearly dominate every panel he appears in. This was intended to be a *Holmes* tale from the start, not a vampire melodrama, so Dracula's role is restrained to a minimum. In a future date I would very much like to return to the Lord of the Undead. I feel he still has a tale to be told.

There have been many requests for a sequel to *Scarlet In Gaslight*, but, I fear, Sherlock Holmes will never meet Dracula again; although this does not mean that I am done with The Great Detective. For me there is hardly a character and a world as fascinating, and already Seppo and I have begun work on a new mini-series, *A Case of Blind Fear*, setting Holmes against H.G. Wells' Invisible Man. The first issue should be in comic stores this December.

My conscience wouldn't let me sign off without properly acknowledging and thanking certain folk: my gratitude first goes to Dame Jean Conan Doyle who so kindly authorized *Scarlet* into the Holmes mythos; the help and encouragement given me by co-plotter Wayne R. Smith—who was always there to suggest a good idea when I could only think of bad ones; my warmest compliments to artist Seppo Makinen, who met the deadlines heroically through an unexpected illness; for Mike Sopp—who got Seppo and I together; a special thanks to Ray Bradbury who believed in me; an appreciation to my wife Martha—sharing our life with Mr. Holmes isn't always a pleasant circumstance; and finally to Chris Ulm and Brian Marshall who took a chance and made a writer very happy.

I can think of nothing more appropriate to my feelings regarding *Scarlet* than closing with Conan Doyle's own sentiment regarding his fiction:

> "I have wrought my simple plan
> If I bring one hour of joy
> To the boy who's half a man
> Or the man who's half a boy."

Martin Powell
June 6, 1988
Louisville, KY

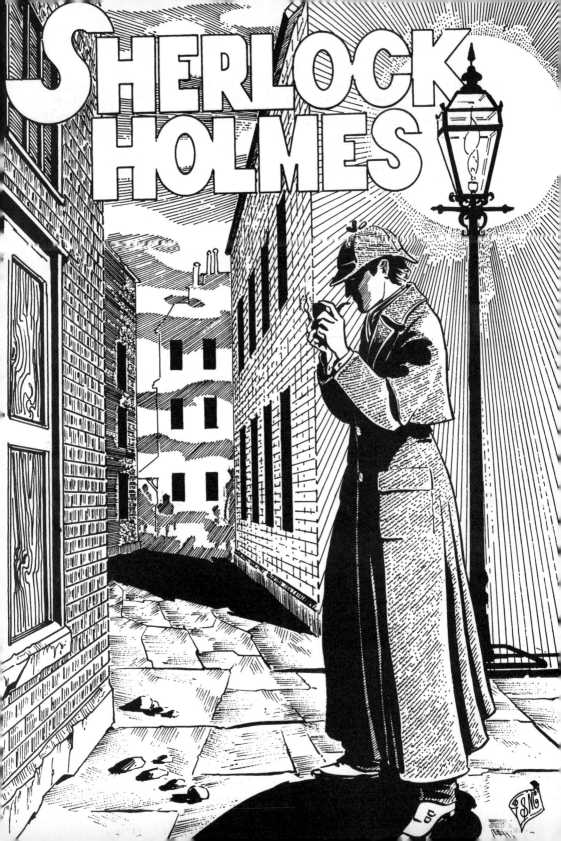

CRASH!

TRANSYLVANIA.

PROLOGUE II: DESTINATION.

③

DOCTOR.

DR. VAN HELSING! I'VE READ YOUR MONOGRAPHS ON RARE DISEASES WITH MUCH ENTHUSIASM, SIR!

I BEG YOUR PARDON, SIR! WE ARE MR. SHERLOCK HOLMES AND DR. WATSON, HERE AT MRS. WESTENRA'S REQUEST.

AH, THE *FAMOUS* DETECTIVE! I HAVE LONGED TO MEET YOU, HERR HOLMES. DR. ABRAHAM VAN HELSING AT YOUR SERVICE.

I AM *HONORED*, DOCTOR. AND I AM, OF COURSE, FAMILIAR WITH YOUR ACCOUNTS OF YOUR FRIEND'S CASES.

I--I'M ALL RIGHT NOW, DOCTOR, I HOPE YOU ARE NOT ANGRY THAT I CALLED MR. HOLMES HERE.

NOT AT ALL. I *WELCOME* THE AID FROM SUCH A BRILLIANT SOURCE.

FOLLOW ME, GENTLEMEN. HER POOR MOTHER SUFFERS FROM A WEAK HEART, BUT MISS LUCY...

...HAS IMPROVED MUCH SINCE MY ARRIVAL.

MISS LUCY, I BRING YOU TWO VERY FAMOUS VISITORS, MR. SHERLOCK HOLMES AND DR. WATSON.

THEN, YOU HAVE MADE A DIAGNOSIS?

PERHAPS, I HAVE TAKEN, AH *PRECAUTIONS*.

GOOD AFTERNOON, MISS WESTENRA.

OH! HOW EXCITING!

MAY WE SEE THE YOUNG PATIENT, DOCTOR?

THESE GENTLEMEN ARE HERE TO HELP YOU, MY DEAR, WITH YOUR-- AH, *NIGHTMARES*.

I'VE READ OF YOUR ADVENTURES FOR *YEARS*.

BUT I HAVEN'T HAD ANY OTHERS, NOT SINCE YOU'VE BEEN HERE, DR. VAN HELSING.

THAT'S A RELIEF TO HEAR MISS WESTENRA. ANY DIZZINESS? NAUSEA?

AND AS EACH DAY PASSES, I REMEMBER THEM LESS.

HMMM? WILD GARLIC? WINDOWS *NAILED* SHUT?

10

AN INQUISITIVE CREATURE... A BEAUTIFUL CREATURE.

HER HAIR... HER EYES. THE SAME DANGEROUS EYES. I HAD ALMOST FORGOTTEN. SO MUCH ALIKE, SO LOVELY.

SO DEADLY.

WE'D BEST LEAVE NOW, HOLMES. WE DON'T WANT TO TIRE HER.

HOLMES! ARE YOU ALLRIGHT?

IT'S NOTHING, WATSON. A TRIFLE WARM, PERHAPS.

THAT IS ALL.

SHE IS NOT THE SAME, I KNOW. SHE CAN'T BE. AND YET...

SO MUCH ALIKE...

GENTLEMEN, YOU'RE LEAVING?

HOWEVER, I CAUTION YOU TO LOCK ALL THE DOORS AND WINDOWS TONIGHT.

WHY THE OMINOUS WARNING HOLMES? THE GIRL IS RECOVERING ADMIRABLY.

AND SHOULD YOU NEED US, A LAMP IN MISS LUCY'S WINDOW WILL SPEED US HERE FROM THE INN.

THERE IS MORE TO THIS THAN ILLNESS, MY FRIEND. YOU NOTICED THE WOUNDS ON MISS LUCY'S THROAT?

YOUR DAUGHTER IS RECOVERING WELL, MADAM. SHE WILL BE HERSELF IN NO TIME.

THANK YOU, MR. HOLMES. TONIGHT I SHALL SLEEP AT EASE.

WOUNDS? WHY, NO!

YES, NEAR THE JUGULAR.

12

SHE IS STRIKING IN THE MOONLIGHT, WADING THROUGH THE BROKEN SHARDS...

...IN ALL THE AGES PAST I HAVE NEVER KNOWN ONE SUCH AS SHE—

MY HEART QUICKENS AS IT HAS NOT IN FIFTY DECADES.

LEAVING A RUBY TRAIL BEHIND.

MY COLD FLESH ACHES FOR HER TREMBLING TOUCH, MY NOSTRILS HUNGER FOR THE PERFUME OF HER BREATH.

SHE SIGHS LIKE A CRADLED CHILD. THE DWELLING IS BLUE WITH DEATH.

BUT SHE RUNS RED...

...WITH LIFE.

16

THROUGH THE WALLS, IN THE QUIET OF THE PLACE, I *FEEL* HER...THE GENTLE SLOPE OF HER SHOULDERS, THE WOMANLY CURVE OF HER HIPS...

YOU SHOULD SEE ME DANCE THE POLKA-- YOU SHOULD SEE ME COVER THE GROUND... LA-LA LA-LA LA-LA

ALTHOUGH NOT IN THE ROOM--NOT YET--I AM *THERE*... THE TOUCHING IS *REAL*.

SHE DOES NOT KNOW.

FOR THE ROLLICKING-- FROLLICKING POLKA IS THE JOLLIEST DANCE A-ROUND.

WELL JANEY-GIRL...YA AIN'T 'ALF BAD, YA AIN'T. NOBODY'D KNOW I'D BE HITTIN' ME THIRTY-MARK TOMOR-RAW!

I HEAR ALL OF HER...THE *PUMP* AND *FLOW* AND *POUNDING* RHYTHM WITHIN THE PRECIOUS SHELL.

A LIT'LE EXTRA PAINT AND POWDER...THAT'S ALL IT TAKES...

THAT YOU, "JOHNNY"? A BIT EARLY... I AIN'T DECENT YET...

UNLIKE THE WOMAN, MY CONSCIOUSNESS IS NOT CONTAINED WITHIN ME...I AM ALL ABOUT HER, IN THE ROOM, IN HER THOUGHTS-- *EVERYWHERE*.

I CATCH HER SCENT WITHOUT BREATHING...SEE THE BLUE OF HER EYES WITHOUT LOOKING...

...BUT I GUESS IF IT WAS *DECENCY* YA WAS AFTER YA WOULDN'T BE HERE--EH? HA!

WELL--? WATCHA HIDIN' IN THE 'ALL FOR? C'MON IN AND CLOSE THE DOOR.

...KNOW HER EARLIEST MEMORIES, HER DEAREST DREAMS.

AND HER DEEPEST *PASSIONS*.

"JOHNNY"...?

WE HAVE NEVER MET...

...AND I KNOW HER *COMPLETELY*.

OH! YA GIMME A FRIGHT, YA DID! HOW'S COME YA'RE CREEPIN' ABOUT ALL QUIET AND...

'EY! HOW'S COME I CAN'T SEE YA IN THE GLASS?

1

LEAVE HER BODY IN THE WHITECHAPEL AREA...AND TAKE CARE TO SLASH HER THROAT AND MUTILATE THE ABDOMEN--AS DONE THE *OTHERS*.

GET DR. CREAM TO DO IT... I WANT THIS TO LOOK LIKE THE *RIPPER'S* WORK.

THIS KIND OF "SERVICE" IS *DEGRADING*. I AM A WAR-RIOR, A *HUNTER*. NOT A *RAPIST*.

THIS IS NOT THE WILDS OF *TRANSYLVANIA*, COUNT. LONDON HAS LAWS AGAINST KILLING PEOPLE IN THE STREETS.

OUR *ACCOMODA-TIONS* FOR YOU WILL BE UPHELD.

I AM NOT YOUR *SLAVE*, PROFES-SOR MORIARTY

I SHOULD NEVER HAVE LEFT WHITBY--ABANDONING MY BELOVED LUCY TO THE *BUTCHERY* OF *VAN HELSING*. SHE WOULD BE WITH ME NOW, HAD I NOT ANSWERED YOUR CALL.

NEVER FORGET IT WAS *I* WHO MASTER-MINDED YOUR JOURNEY TO ENGLAND.

YES. THE GIRL. I SUSPECTED AS MUCH.

I ASSURE YOU, SIR, I WAS AS *DISMAYED* AS YOU BY THE GIRL'S BRUTAL MURDER. HAD NOT ONE OF MY MOST TRUSTED MEN *WITNESSED* THE GRISLY EPISODE, I SHOULD NOT BELIEVE A DOC-TOR WITH ABRAHAM VAN HELSING'S REPUTATION CAPABLE OF SUCH *SAVAGRY*.

A *WOODEN STAKE* WAS USED TO PIERCE THE TORSO, I BELIEVE.

MY LUCY'S BLOOD WARMS ME STILL... IT IS NOT EASY TO BELIEVE SHE IS *DEAD*.

BUT--IF ALIVE-- SHE WOULD HAVE SOUGHT ME OUT...*CALLED* TO ME... JOINED AT MY SIDE.

I HAVE *LISTENED*... BUT THERE IS ONLY SILENCE.

I WAS... *DISPLEASED* AS YOU LINGERED IN WHITBY-- AGAINST MY ORDERS. IT WAS ONLY YOUR CHANCE MEETING WITH HOLMES THAT SAVED YOU IN MY EYES.

MY SPIES TELL ME HE WAS DRIVEN QUITE *MAD* FROM THE EN-COUNTER. THIS PLEASES ME ENOUGH TO FORGIVE YOU.

I AM *IMMUNE* FROM YOUR THREATS, MORIARTY.

4

WAIT FOR ME, CABBY.

I WON'T BE LONG.

AYE, SAH.

221B

KNOCK KNOCK

MYCROFT HOLMES! I APPRECIATE YOUR COMING AT SUCH SHORT NOTICE. I KNOW YOU HAVE A *DISLIKE* FOR STREET-TRAVEL.

NONSENSE, DR. WATSON. COME--LET US NOT TALK *OUTSIDE.*

I WAS AT *PARLIAMENT* UPON RECEIVING YOUR WIRE... AND WAS PURPOSELY *DETAINED* IN MY SPEED OF TRAVEL. *SOMEONE,* IT SEEMS, DID NOT WISH MY PRESENCE IN BAKER STREET TONIGHT.

MORIARTY?

UNLESS I AM *MUCH* MISTAKEN.

THEN-- HOLMES WAS RIGHT ABOUT HIM WATCHING HIS EVERY MOVE. *INCREDIBLE.*

THE THOUGHT OF A *"NAPOLEON OF CRIME"* IS TERRIFYING.

IT CAN RAISE GOOSEFLESH ON THE *IGNORANT--* BUT I HAVEN'T VERY PROBABLY RISKED MY *LIFE* TONIGHT TO DISCUSS THE EVILS OF THE LONDON UNDERWORLD. SO, DOCTOR...

...HOW LONG HAS MY BROTHER BEEN *ILL?*

THE *BRAIN FEVER* HAS GROWN WORSE THE PAST-- *WAIT A MOMENT!* I MADE NO MENTION OF HOLMES' SICKNESS IN MY WIRE...HOW COULD YOU POSSIBLY KNOW--

TUT-TUT, DOCTOR-- I HAVE NO *TIME...* YOUR NERVOUS AGITATION, THE ODD URGENCY OF YOUR CABLE, THE FRESH STAIN OF OPIUM UPON YOUR CUFF... I'D BE DULL INDEED IF I WERE NOT AT ONCE CONCERNED WITH MY BROTHER'S *HEALTH.*

REMARKABLE.

YOU'RE *RIGHT--*ON ALL COUNTS. HOLMES IS SEVERELY ILL. THE DILUTED OPIUM HELPS, BUT ONLY BRIEFLY. I FEAR GIVING HIM HEAVIER DOSES BECAUSE OF THE... OTHER SUBSTANCE ABUSES HE--

CRASH

QUICKLY DOCTOR-- BEFORE HE HARMS HIMSELF!

⑦

8

HE'S BEEN *RANTING* FOR DAYS ABOUT THIS MYSTERIOUS WOMAN... KEPT INSISTING THAT YOU WOULD UNDERSTAND.

REGRETTABLY, I DO NOT.

...ONLY YOU... MYCROFT... ONLY YOU CAN SAVE ME...

WILL YOU...? *WILL YOU...?*

OF COURSE I WILL, SHERLOCK. NEVER FEAR... SHE, AH, IS GONE. *I SWEAR.* YOU ARE SAFE NOW.

SAFE...? SAFE...

LET'S COME AWAY... HE'LL SLEEP SOON.

VERY WELL. I SHALL RETURN TO LOOK IN ON YOU, SHERLOCK. *REST* NOW. YOU MUST GET WELL.

...AND... YOU WILL NOT LET HER COME... MYCROFT? YOU PROMISE...?

I *PROMISE.* I WILL *PROTECT* YOU.

HE'S FINALLY *OUT*, POOR SOUL. I WILL GIVE HIM THE BEST CARE POSSIBLE, MR. HOLMES.

I KNOW YOU WILL, DOCTOR. MY BROTHER IS MOST FORTUNATE TO HAVE SUCH A *FRIEND.*

"I WILL EXPECT REGULAR REPORTS, DR. WATSON."

"CERTAINLY. I'LL WRITE DAILY UPON HIS CONDITION...

...AND YOU MUSTN'T WORRY -- HE'LL SLEEP THE REST OF THE NIGHT."

"THANK YOU FOR COMING, MR. HOLMES -- I DOUBT I COULD HAVE *CALMED* HIM WITHOUT YOU."

"NOT AT ALL... IT IS MY *BUSINESS*..."

"WE ARE A FAMILY AFTER ALL..."

"...AND HAVE BEEN THROUGH *MUCH* TOGETHER."

9

I DID NOT KNOW MYCROFT HOLMES *WELL*, BUT I CONFESS TO AN ODD SENSE OF CALM MELANCHOLY AFTER HIS VISIT.

HE HAD ACCOMPLISHED WHAT I COULD NOT, PRODUCING A SOOTHING EFFECT UPON HOLMES THAT WAS, COMPARED TO MY LACK OF SUCCESS OVER THE PAST SEVERAL DAYS, ONLY SOMEWHAT SHORT OF *SPECTACULAR*.

I'LL ADMIT TO A GUILTY FEELING OF JEALOUSY REGARDING THE BROTHERS' MARKED *RAPPORT*... BUT I WAS PLEASED MY FRIEND HAD BEEN EASED, IF ONLY A LITTLE, OF HIS AGONY.

OF COURSE, I HAD TOLD MYCROFT HOLMES NOTHING OF OUR *"VAMPIRE ADVENTURE."* HE WAS A VERY IMPORTANT MAN AT PARLIAMENT, AND PERHAPS EVEN SUPERIOR TO HIS MORE FAMOUS BROTHER IN MATTERS OF MIND AND REASON...

IT WOULDN'T DO TO TELL SUCH A MAN TALES OF *BLOODSUCKING* GHOSTS.

DR. WATSON! PARDON MY INTRUSION-- I SAW YOUR LIGHTS... I MUST SPEAK WITH YOU!

IT IS *VERY LATE*, DR. VAN HELSING...

JA, I APOLOGIZE FOR THE HOUR-- BUT I *NEED* TO CONSULT WITH HERR HOLMES *DESPERATELY*.

HOLMES HAS BEEN VERY ILL SINCE THE... *INCIDENT* AT WHITBY. I'M AFRAID WHAT YOU ASK IS *IMPOSSIBLE*.

IF SO, THIS CITY-- JA, THIS NATION IS DOOMED.

HOLMES MUST BE BROUGHT INTO THIS-- THERE IS WORK, *WILD WORK* TO BE DONE!

JUST *WHAT* ARE YOU TALKING ABOUT?

IT IS MY FAULT... MINE ALONE... I TAKE THE FULL BLAME. YET I CAN NOT STOP THIS HORROR I HAVE LET LOOSE...

SPEAK PLAINLY! WHAT "HORROR"? WHAT *HAPPENED*?

LUCY WESTENRA... SHE IS ALIVE IN THIS CITY-- AS A *VAMPIRE*.

GOTT HELP ME.

⑩

I DON'T UNDERSTAND. YOU WERE GOING TO PUT HER AT *REST*. THE STAKE...

JA, JA-- AND I WAS THERE BEFORE SUNDOWN... BUT HER BODY WAS GONE FROM THE CRYPT ALREADY.

GONE? IN THE *DAYLIGHT?*

I CAN NOT EXPLAIN IT MYSELF. REGARDLESS-- WE MUST *STOP* HER, DR. WATSON. *WE MUST!*

WHAT CAN I DO?

NO ONE WILL BELIEVE ME--NOT SCOTLAND YARD... *NO ONE.* YOU CAN HELP ME *CONVINCE* THEM.

I KNOW THE *DANGER*, DR. VAN HELSING, AND WILL HELP ANYWAY I CAN.

THANK YOU, SIR. I ONLY PRAY IT HASN'T YET *STARTED*. THE VAMPIRE PLAGUE SPREADS FAST. MANY WILL FALL PREY TO THE BLOOD-LUST--WHILE OTHERS ARE *INFUSED* WITH THE CREATURE'S OWN TAINTED BLOOD... BECOMING MONSTERS *THEMSELVES*.

THIS WAS THE CASE WITH *MISS LUCY*.

"THEN YOU EXPECT AN *EPIDEMIC!* HOW WILL IT START?"

"I'VE SPENT A LIFETIME IN SCRUTINY OF THESE BEINGS... WHETHER IN EUROPE, AFRICA OR THE ORIENT-- THE SYMPTOMS REMAIN THE SAME.

"IT ALWAYS STARTS *SMALL*...

"...VAGUE...

"...ALMOST *UNNOTICED*.

TAP TAP!

"UNTIL IT IS *THERE*...

"...AND YOU CAN IGNORE IT *NO MORE*."

"THEY ARE CLEVER. THE PROMISES--THE *LIES* FOOL MANY.

"IN THEIR *AWESOME* SCOPE OF ABILITIES, THERE ARE TWO *SUBTLE* DECEPTIONS MOST EFFECTIVE.

"...THEY ARE *NOT* WHAT THEY SEEM...

"...AND WE WILL NOT *BELIEVE* IN THEM.

"AND--BY THE TIME YOUR AUTHORITIES DISCOVER THE *TRUTH*...

CLICK!

"...IT IS ALREADY *TOO LATE.*"

12

THE ATTACKER IS LONG GONE.

NO MATTER.

QUITE A PERFORMANCE ON MY PART.

SORRY OLD FRIEND.

I COULDN'T ENDANGER YOU FURTHER.

MORIARTY DOESN'T WANT *YOU*.

IT IS *I* HE WANTS.

INTERESTING, THAT BEGGAR'S TEETH WERE AMAZINGLY *CANINE*.

IF VAN HELSING'S THEORY THAT COULD SUGGEST AN EVOLUTIONARY ADAPT--

HELLO... *WHAT'S THIS?*

BLOOD.

A TRAIL OF IT.

FRESH.

YOU THERE--! ARE YOU INJURED? DO YOU NEED--

GOD IN HEAVEN.

IT CAN NOT BE.

WATSON PRONOUNCED HER DEAD...ATTENDED HER FUNERAL.

LUCY WESTENRA.

YOU REMEMBER ME...I'M FLATTERED.

I RECALL FROM YOUR TALES THAT YOU NORMALLY NOTICE YOUNG LADIES...

STAY AWAY FROM ME--

...BUT I AM NOT LIKE THE OTHERS-- AM I, MR. HOLMES?

NOT AT ALL LIKE THEM.

PLEASE... DON'T...

COME--LET ME SHOW YOU!

DO YOU SEE... DETECTIVE--?

I AM EVERY- THING YOU'VE EVER DREAMT OF.

NO... NO! KEEP AWAY!

17

20

THOSE *SHOTS*--! THERE! *IT'S* HOLMES!

HOLMES! STAND WHERE YOU ARE!

TAKE CARE, DOCTOR!

IT CAN DO NOTHING WHILE I HAVE *THIS*!

VAN HELSING!

YOU HAVE INTERFERED THE FINAL TIME!

GONE--INTO THE FOG! *VANISHED! INCREDIBLE!*

THEN YOU *SAW* THEM, WATSON! *BOTH OF THEM?*

CALM YOURSELF, MY FRIEND IT IS *OVER.*

OVER! HA! IT HAS JUST *BEGUN!*

ALL IS *RIGHT* AS *RAIN!*

HOLMES? YOU AREN'T YOURSELF.

I ASSURE YOU, MY DEAR WATSON, I AM PERFECTLY *FIT*-- THE FEVER HAS PASSED. AT LAST-- *BRAIN-WORK!*

WHAT CONVINCES YOU NOW, HERR HOLMES, THAT THIS EPISODE-- LIKE YOUR PREVIOUS ENCOUNTER-- IS NOT A MERE HALLUCINATION?

SIMPLICITY ITSELF, VAN HELSING.

WHEN YOU HAVE ELIMINATED THE IMPOSSIBLE, WHATEVER REMAINS-- HOWEVER IMPROBABLE-- *MUST BE THE TRUTH!*

THIS GOWN IS NO ILLUSION, GENTLEMEN.

NOR THE FRESH *BLOOD* ON IT.

21

VAMPIRIC BLOOD! DO YOU REALIZE THE OPPORTUNITY THIS PRESENTS?

I DO INDEED. WE SHALL KNOW THEM INTIMATELY NOW-- DOWN TO THE VERY BIOLOGY OF THEIR UNIQUE METABOLISM.

IT'S WONDERFUL HAVING YOU BACK, OLD FRIEND.

I OWE YOU MY LIFE, WATSON...

...AND TO YOU, DOCTOR VAN HELSING.

COME--WE MUST WORK QUICKLY... "KNOWLEDGE IS OUR MOST POTENT WEAPON."

HA, HA! WELL SPOKEN HERR HOLMES.

Journal entry 8 April, 1891.

The end of the truce is near. Have doubled the evening guards accordingly.

I feel he will come tonight. I am prepared. The only difficult thing is the waiting.

I have never been a PATIENT man.

On to more vital items.

The French serum has failed. Anna feels I should have continued the treatments for another month. We don't HAVE another month.

22

Received word this evening that the American specialist is willing to discuss terms.

Ruby is taking good care of his infant son until such time he developes a cure.

He has *TWO WEEKS*.

Ah...

He has arrived as expected.

TRAITOR!

YOU HAVE USED ME, MORIARTY... MADE A MOCKERY OF MY HONOUR.

OUR ALLIANCE IS FINISHED.

AS ARE YOU-- AHHHHH!

I AM READY FOR THIS VISIT, COUNT. AS YOU CAN SEE.

SO--YOU'VE SEEN YOUR PRECIOUS LUCY. TOO BAD. I DIDN'T WISH OUR COLLABORATION TO END SO SUDDENLY.

I *NEEDED* THE GIRL, YOU SEE... A CREATURE OF *YOUR BLOOD*-- YET MORE PLIABLE TO MY WILL.

IT WAS A SIMPLE MATTER, BRINGING HER BODY HERE AFTER *BURIAL*.

23

THE CROSS WILL NOT SAVE YOU. A THOUSAND MEN FELL BY MY HAND *CENTURIES* BEFORE YOU WERE BORN.

I NEED NOT *TOUCH* YOU--

TOUCHE.

--TO *KILL* YOU!

BANG BANG

AAAARRRGGHH!

IT IS THE STING OF PURE *SILVER* THAT YOU FEEL... DISSOLVING IN YOUR BLOOD, THE LETHAL GRAINS RACING THROUGH YOUR VEINS.

I REGRET THIS ACTION. GENUINELY, I DO. YOU WERE A FORMIDABLE ALLY, COUNT DRACULA.

MUCH TOO DANGEROUS TO *LIVE*.

24

SHE WAS QUITE *LOVELY*...THE LITTLE STREET WOMAN.

I HAD FOLLOWED HER ALL EVENING, ALTHOUGH SHE NEVER HEARD MY GENTLE TREAD.

I WAS THERE WHEN SHE SPOKE SOFTLY TO THE GENTLEMAN ON THE DIMLY-LIGHTED CORNER.

HER *BREATH* WAS LIKE WATER FLOWERS...ALL THROATY AND *WET*.

I WATCHED HER ENTER HIS CARRIAGE...WATCHED *PAINFULLY* AS THEY COUPLED AND THEN DREW APART, CHILLED BY THEIR SUDDEN SWEAT.

OVER HIS SHOULDER I WATCHED AS HE TOOK HER HOME, UN-LOCKING HER DOOR AS A GENTLEMAN SHOULD.

THERE WAS A *CARNAL* REEK WITHIN THE PLACE THAT ASSURED ME THAT THIS WAS NO LIVING NICHE... ALTHOUGH SHE SLEPT THERE...

...THIS WAS NO *HOME*. I ENTERED EASILY, UNINVITED.

HE WAS A LITTLE DRUNK, A LITTLE LOUD. "QUIET," SHE WHISPERED, "YOU'LL WAKE MY..." AND I FOUND *IT*.

HOW *WONDERFUL*. I LEFT THEM BOTH STILL, *COLD*-- A FROST SHIM-MERING UPON THEIR SKINS.

FAR ABOVE I THINK I HEAR THE *THUNDER* OF A TEMPEST...

...OR IS IT THE *WILD BEATING* OF MY *HEART*?

①

3

WELL... WHAT 'AVE WE GOT 'ERE?

I'LL BE--! A COUPLE OF LUCKY NIPPERS IS WHAT WE ARE!

WHY--IT'S THE OLD GENT HISSELF!

LET ME ALONE.

4

OLD IS RIGHT. LOOKS LIKE ME LOST POPPA!

THERE IS HURT IN THE LAUGHTER, A HARDNESS TO THEIR EYES. I KNOW THESE MEN, MORIARTY'S MINIONS... FROM THE TRANSFUSION ROOM.

RATHER.

I HAVE SEALED MY OWN FATE.

ANGER.

GREED.

ENVY.

LET'S SAY 'ELLO TO OUR OLD DAD!

THEIR HATRED POURS UPON ME...

...LIKE WASTED BLOOD.

HA HA HA HA

WE ARE MASTER HERE!

HE CAN DO NOTHING-- LONDON IS OURS!

ENJOY THE SUNRISE, OLD MAN... BEEN A LONG WHILE SINCE YE'VE SEEN IT!

THE SUN...

...ALREADY--?

5

<THANK YOU FOR A MOST *INVIGORATING* EXPERIENCE, SARAH. I'VE NEVER BEFORE ATTENDED AN *ALL-NIGHT* REHEARSAL!*>

<I HOPE YOUR POOR SECRETARY WASN'T TOO *BORED*. HE'S BEEN SO *QUIET* ALL EVENING.>

<*NONSENSE!* HE IS AT HOME IN THE THEATRE--HE IS SIMPLY *EMBARRASSED* BY HIS WEAK COMMAND OF YOUR BEAUTIFUL LANGUAGE!>

<HA! BETTER THAN *MY* ENGLISH, I'LL WAGER! GOOD MORNING, HENRY. I'LL SEE YOU AFTER TONIGHT'S PERFORMANCE.>

*TRANSLATED FROM THE FRENCH.

<MOTHER'S *HOME*, FELENA! DID YOU MISS ME!>

<WHAT IS WRONG, DEAREST? YOU ARE *TREMBLING*...>

<WHAT IS THIS...? *BLOOD?*>

<GUSTAVE...IF THIS IS ANOTHER TRICK--->

SARAH... HELP ME.

8

...AND--JUDGING FROM THESE **ODOROUS** CHEMICALS-- IT SEEMS HERR HOLMES HAS SHARED MY INSOMNIA.

HA! TRUE ENOUGH, ABRAHAM. THERE'S NO HOPE IN GETTING **ANY-THING** OUT OF HIM JUST YET, SO...

...WHY DON'T **WE** DISCOVER WHAT CULINARY CONCOCTIONS MRS. HUDSON HAS PREPARED THIS--

I'M QUITE FINISHED, WATSON. GOOD MORNING, DR. VAN HELSING. FROM YOUR EXPRESSION I SUSPECT YOU'VE **NEWS** FOR US?

JA, HERR HOLMES, A FRUITFUL NIGHT'S INVESTIGATION. I DISCOVERED--NOT ONLY ONE OF OUR ENEMY'S HIDING PLACES--BUT HIS **IDENTITY,** AND POINT OF ORIGIN--

TRANSYLVANIA, PERHAPS?

HOW--?!

ON THE **CONTRARY.**

I DON'T UNDERSTAND! I WAS **ALL NIGHT** GATHERING THAT INFORMATION... HOW COULD YOU **POSSIBLY** KNOW?

NO MAGIC, DOCTOR. THE SAMPLE OF **SOIL** I FOUND IN MISS WESTENRA'S BEDROOM WAS CLEARLY **NOT** ENGLISH EARTH. IN REFERRING TO MY THREE MONOGRAPHS ON THE SOIL AND CLAY OF BRITAIN AND CENTRAL EUROPE, I WAS ABLE TO LOCATE THE REGION IN ONLY A FEW HOURS.

EXTRAORDINARY.

"COMMONPLACE, DOCTOR, ONE NEEDS MERELY TO KNOW WHERE TO LOOK. NOW THEN, YOU HAVE MORE TO OFFER US?"

"JA, I BELIEVE SO... MY MANY INTERVIEWS OF THE DAY CLIMAXED IN MY MEETING A MR. PETER HAWKINS--A LOCAL SOLICITOR.

"IT WAS **HIS** OFFICE THAT HAD HANDLED THE SHIPPING ARRANGEMENTS FOR THE FIFTY WOODEN BOXES ABOARD **THE DEMETER.** THE CRATES WERE INVOICED AS CONTAINING **MOLD.** THEIR DESTINATION WAS **WHITBY.** THE ENTIRE CARGO OWNED BY A NOBLEMAN, ORIGINATING FROM **TRANSYLVANIA.**

"BY NIGHTFALL I HAD TRACED A DOZEN OF THE BOXES TO A HOUSE HERE IN LONDON--A RUINED ESTATE CALLED CARFAX ABBEY.

"I WISH I COULD DESCRIBE THE **VILE** ATMOSPHERE OF THE PLACE. EVERY EVIL BREATH FROM THAT **MONSTER** CLUNG TO THE VERY WALLS AND RAFTERS.

"IF ONLY YOU COULD FEEL THE UNEARTHLY **MOOD** OF THE AWFUL PLACE--PARTICULARLY AT **NIGHT...**

"...BUT IT HAD BEEN LONG DARK WHEN I ARRIVED AND THUS I WAS CERTAIN THE **MASTER** OF THE ABBEY WOULD NOT BE THERE.

"I KNEW THIS, YET...

"...SOMEHOW...

"...I FELT NOT **ALONE.**"

G'EVEN', SAH. DIDN'T MEAN TA *SCARE* YE...

WHAT DO YOU WANT? WHAT ARE YOU DOING HERE?!

COULD YE SPARE A COPPER FER OL' ROSINE, SAH?

YOU HAVEN'T ANSWERED ME. WHY ARE YOU IN THIS *TERRIBLE* PLACE?

TERRIBLE--IS IT? POOR OL' ROSINE DON'T KNOW IT FROM WINDSOR PALACE...GOTS TA KEEP THE WIND OFF ME BACKSIDE, Y'KNOW...'TIS A FINE, BIG HOUSE...

UH, SO 'BOUTS ME COPPERS, SAH?

SURELY, YOU MUST HAVE A *HOME*, MADAME--?

HOME? OL' ROSINE'S GOTS HOMES ALL OVER... ON HARLEY STREET AND OXFORD AND--

OOOOOOOH

MADAME!

IT-IT'S JEST THE DIZZIES, SAH...CAIN'T 'MEMBER WHEN ME LAST MEAL WAS.

HERE, MY GOOD MADAME-- THERE'S ENOUGH FOR A WARM BED AND A GOOD BREAKFAST IN THE MORNING. BUT YOU MUST PROMISE TO STAY AWAY FROM THIS HOUSE... IT IS *DANGEROUS* IN WAYS YOU WOULDN'T UNDERSTAND.

AHHH! GOD BLESS YOU FOR A GENTLEMAN!

'ANGELS AND MINISTERS OF GRACE DEFEND US'!

"EXCUSE ME, DOCTOR. ARE YOU CERTAIN SHE SAID THOSE *EXACT* WORDS?"

"I AM, HERR HOLMES. IT SEEMED *ODD* TO ME AT THE TIME...STRANGELY *FAMILIAR*."

"INDEED. IT IS A DIRECT QUOTE--ACT I, SCENE IV, OF *HAMLET*."

"AH, OF COURSE! I'D HEARD IT *BEFORE*. CURIOUS THAT SUCH A PITIFUL CREATURE WOULD COMMIT SHAKESPEARE TO MEMORY."

"QUITE SO. PLEASE CONTINUE."

AFTER WATCHING HER LEAVE SAFELY, I PROCEEDED TO *SANCTIFY* THE COFFINS WITH HOLY WATER, SO NOW THE MONSTER CAN NO LONGER FIND SHELTER AT CARFAX. OF COURSE THERE ARE MANY MORE COFFINS TO FIND--AND *DESTROY*.

INTERESTING, DOCTOR--BUT YOU HAVE NEGLECTED TO *NAME* THIS MYSTERIOUS TRANSYLVANIAN NOBLEMAN.

HOW CLUMSY OF ME! I AM NOT USED TO RELATING ADVENTURES. HIS NAME IS *COUNT DRACULA*.

DRACULA? HMMM.

⑪

YOUR ACCOUNT OF THE OLD WOMAN IS INTRIGUING, VAN HELSING. I FEAR THIS *DRACULA* WILL HAVE *ANOTHER* PLACE TO REST TODAY BECAUSE OF HER.

WHAT DO YOU MEAN, HOLMES?

I OBSERVE A SLIGHT STAIN OF *GREASEPAINT* ON THIS SLEEVE-- FROM YOUR HANDS BRUSHING TO- GETHER AS SHE TOOK THE COINS, NO DOUBT. THE WOMAN WAS AN *ACTRESS* ARRANGED TO DUPE YOU, VAN HELSING.

BUT--BUT TO WHAT PURPOSE?

HMMM. THE FAINT- ING ACT MAY BE THE CLUE. FALLING AGAINST THE OPEN COFFIN, SHE WAS ABLE TO SMUGGLE AWAY ONE OR TWO HANDFULS OF THE FOREIGN EARTH INTO HER GARMENTS...

...WITH NO OTHER MOTIVE BUT TO CREATE, BY PROXY, ANOTHER *"GRAVE"* FOR OUR VAMPIRE.

JA, HERR HOLMES. YOUR REASONING IS *CLEAR.* I WAS BLIND-- *STUPID.*

NOT AT ALL, DOCTOR. REMEMBER, WE ARE DEALING WITH AN EXTREMELY CUNNING FOE--THE SOIL-FILLED BOXES ATTEST TO HIS *GENIUS.* HE ANTICIPATES OUR EVERY MOVE. WE MUST BE *CARE- FUL.* READY, WATSON?

WHERE ARE WE GOING?

THE BRITISH MUSEUM. IT'S HIGH TIME WE LEARNED SOME- THING ABOUT *COUNT DRACULA.*

I SUGGEST YOU CONTINUE YOUR SEARCH FOR THE REMAINING BOXES, DR. VAN HELSING...

....AND, I THINK, YOU WILL APPRECIATE THE *IRONY* IN THE ANSWERS REVEALED FROM YES- TERDAY'S TELEGRAMS. IT SEEMS THE ENTIRE VOYAGE AND CARGO OF THE DEMETER WAS FINANCED BY A MR. "MORTIMER JAMES" OF LONDON.

MORTIMER JAMES-- AH! THAT WOULD BE YOUR NORTORIOUS PROFESSOR *JAMES MORIARTY,* I PRESUME?

UNDOUBTEDLY. THERE IS MORE *EVIL* AFOOT THAN VAMPIRISM, DOCTOR. I FEAR MORIARTY PLANS TO POPULATE LONDON WITH THE PLAGUE-- HIS FINAL REVENGE ON THIS GREAT CITY...

...AND *MYSELF.*

TOGETHER WE WILL STOP HIM, HERR HOLMES! WE WILL MEET AGAIN TOMMOROW, THEN?

IN THE MORNING, DOCTOR. *GOOD HUNTING!*

GOTT BE WITH THE BOTH OF YOU!

12

"IT IS *SUNSET*.

"...YOU PROMISED..."

...IS HE *DEAD?*

HMPH--? AH. *LUCY*. IT IS YOU.

THE NIGHT IS HERE... *ALREADY?*

OBVIOUSLY.

ONCE AGAIN, PROFESSOR MORIARTY--

--IS HE *DEAD?*

13

IS HE? I MUST KNOW!

CALM YOURSELF. THE COUNT IS DESTROYED.

AS I SAID HE WOULD BE.

YOU ARE CERTAIN? ABSOLUTE?

NO VAMPIRE COULD SURVIVE THE SILVER BULLETS I FIRED INTO HIM.

NOT EVEN DRACULA.

THEN... THEN I AM FREE! AT LAST! CLEAR OF HIS SHADOW!

FREE... YES. BEFORE LONG.

"BEFORE LONG"? YOU SAID HE IS DEAD--

AND HE IS. BUT NOW, THE REASON FOR YOUR EXISTENCE HAS COME. THE CRISIS... IS HERE.

AHH... YOU REFER TO THE FAIR AGATHA--?

SHE IS DYING. NOTHING HAS SLOWED THE CONSUMPTION... SHE WILL NOT LIVE THROUGH THE NIGHT.

LUCY...

SHE IS MY ONLY CHILD... I CAN NOT LOSE HER.

I UNDERSTAND, PROFESSOR... BUT WE MUST ACT SWIFTLY-- WHILE THERE IS STILL BREATH IN HER.

OH! YOU STARTLED ME, SIR...

...IT-- IT HAS BECOME... VERY BAD, MISS AGGIE... SHE WON'T AWAKE--

THAT IS ALL FOR NOW, ANNA. COME WITH ME.

SIR-- I... AS YOU SAY, PROFESSOR...

14

"...BUT IS IT PRUDENT, SIR, TO LEAVE MISS AGGIE *ALONE* WITH THAT... *CREATURE?*"

AGATHA.

THE SCENT AND SHADOW OF *DEATH* LINGERS HERE...

...BEHIND THE SHROUDED VEIL.

I DO NOT LIKE THIS PLACE.

THE GLOW OF LIFE FLICKERS...LUNGS RATTLE WITH WEAKNESS...

...DREAMS ARE BLACKENED *NIGHTMARES.*

THE BED IS A COLD TOMB.

HER PASSIVE MORTALITY SICKENS ME... *FRIGHTENS* ME--

--WITH PALE MEMORIES OF WHAT IT IS LIKE TO *DIE.*

I AM MORBIDLY DRAWN TO THE FADING *HOST*--

--AS *DEATH* SWELLS IN THE ROOM.

FATHER...?

I DON'T WANT TO BE HERE.

15

SHE SWEETLY COOS, LIKE AN INFANT...

WHO ARE YOU...? WHERE IS MY FATHER?

... AND THE LOVELY INNOCENCE FILLS ME WITH JOY SO GREAT I COULD **SCREAM.**

DEEPER...**DEEPER** I LOOK INTO POOLS OF SHINING OBSIDIAN...ANSWERING HER IN WAYS ONLY **WE** CAN UNDERSTAND.

PLEASE... TELL ME...

THE FLUTTER OF HER LASHES... THE CURVE OF THE PERFECT LIPS...

...**EVERYTHING** ABOUT HER--

--PULSES THROUGH ME, RACING MY HEART INTO A **WILD HEAT.**

SHE SMILES, KNOWING MY PROMISES ARE REAL.

SHE GROWS COLDER... HER GRAVE BECKONS.

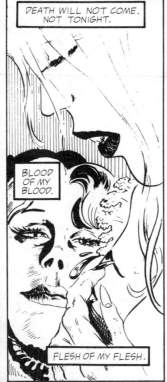

DEATH WILL NOT COME. NOT TONIGHT.

BLOOD OF MY BLOOD.

FLESH OF MY FLESH.

NOT DEATH...

...DEAR ONE.

NOT TONIGHT.

16

THE BRANDY DOESN'T WARM ME.

I'VE DONE ALL I COULD DO FOR HER.

MORE THAN *ANY.*

AGATHA WILL FORGIVE ME. SHE WILL.

SHE *MUST.*

IT IS DONE.

THEN... SHE WILL NOT DIE--?

THERE IS NO DEATH FOR US. I HAVE GIVEN TO AGATHA--AND SHE HAS *TAKEN.*

TOMORROW NIGHT SHE WILL BE WITH YOU.

AND WITH ME.

GO THEN-- LEAVE ME.

I NEED TO BE ALONE NOW. TO THINK.

TO PRAY.

I'VE DONE WHAT I COULD.

MORE THAN ANY.

SHE WILL *UNDERSTAND*... IN TIME.

AGATHA.

GOD.

CRASH!

WHAT HAVE I DONE...?

KRREEKK

17

WHAT IS THIS PLACE?

THE ROOM--THE COFFIN IS *UNFAMILIAR*...

...*THEATRICAL*.

YET MY SACRED *EARTH* PROTECTS ME. THAT-- AND A LIVING SCENT *MOST* COMFORTING.

I REMEMBER.

SARAH.

⟨NEVER FEAR--YOU ARE *SAFE.* I HAVE REMOVED THE BULLETS AND CLEANED THE WOUNDS. THEY ARE HEALING QUICKLY.⟩

⟨TAKE CARE! RISE SLOWLY OR YOU WILL TEAR THEM OPEN.⟩

⟨I...I DON'T KNOW WHAT TO SAY. IF YOU HADN'T RE-TURNED FROM CARFAX WITH THE *EARTH* ON TIME--⟩

⟨HUSH, NOW. HOLD STILL AND LET ME CHANGE THESE... THERE! SEE HOW BETTER THEY LOOK! I AM SURPRISED THAT A SOLDIER BRAVE AS YOU CARRIES SO *FEW* SCARS.⟩

⟨YOU HAVE BEEN... VERY KIND TO ME.⟩

⟨NONSENSE. THE NURSING IS EASY--I HAVE NEVER FORGOTTEN THAT LONG, BLOODY WINTER I SPENT BANDAGING AND CARING FOR THE WOUNDED TROOPS IN PARIS. SUCH THINGS BECOME SECOND NATURE.⟩

⟨YOU ARE IN... GREAT JEOPARDY... I SHOULDN'T STAY.⟩

⟨THE RISK IS MINE.⟩

"⟨SARAH...WHY TAKE SUCH...A CHANCE?⟩"

"⟨IT IS A DEBT REPAYED--A LIFE FOR A *LIFE,* COUNT DRACULA.⟩"

"⟨YOUR CHILDHOOD-- YOUR WHOLE HUMAN LIFE, PROBABLY-- MUST SEEM LITTLE MORE THAN A *DREAM* BY NOW...⟩"

"⟨...BUT TO A LONELY, OFTEN ILL, AND *UN-WANTED* LITTLE GIRL...⟩"

"⟨...THE TIME OF YOUTH TRIGGERS BITTER MEMORIES...⟩"

"⟨...WHEN PEACE WAS FOUND AMONG THE *GRAVES*...AND WHOSE ONLY COMFORT WAS FINDING A FRIEND THAT WOULDN'T PULL AWAY.⟩"

"⟨I GREW MORE AND MORE ILL...SLIPPING OUT INTO THE NIGHT SO AS TO SPEED MY TIME... CONTENTED MY PASSING WOULD MAKE THEM PITY ME... MAKE THEM LOVE ME.⟩"

"⟨I HAD MADE FRIENDS WITH DEATH.⟩"

"⟨I WAS TEN YEARS OLD.⟩"

18

ACCORDING TO THE TRANSYLVANIAN SCHOLAR SZEKLEY, THE DRACULAS WERE KNOWN TO HAVE DEALINGS WITH THE **DEVIL**--WHICH MAY ACCOUNT FOR HIS PECULIAR NATURE. ALTHOUGH THAT IS CERTAINLY SURMISE, AND, IF I MAY SAY SO, A RATHER POOR ONE.

I CAN BELIEVE IT. FROM WHAT I READ THE MAN WAS A **MONSTER**.

AH, HE IS **MUCH** MORE THAN THAT, WATSON. BEFORE MY BELIEFS WERE WERE FLAT-FOOTED UPON THE GROUND-- NO GHOSTS NEED HAVE APPLIED.

AND NOW I AM FACED WITH **THIS**.

I IMAGINE IT **HAS** RATHER OPENED A NEW WORLD TO--

JOVE! WE'VE A BAD STORM COMING, HOLMES! PERHAPS WE SHOULD--

WATSON... **WAIT!** WATSON! HOLD STILL-- LET ME HAVE IT...!

THIS IS IT-- WATSON! **CAN'T** YOU SEE!

IN METRO THEATRE SARAH BERNHARDT IN **HAMLET** ALSO STARRING ELLEN **OPHELIA**

MY GOD, HOLMES! WHAT ON EARTH--?

HURRY! WE'VE NO TIME--**THE GAME IS AFOOT!**

〈HUSH, FELENA.〉

AAH-- WHO...IS IT... PLEASE?

KNOCK KNOCK

GRRRRRR

EXCUSE US, MADAME BERNHARDT... I AM DR. JOHN WATSON-- WITH MY FRIEND **MR. SHERLOCK HOLMES**... I WONDER IF WE MAY HAVE A MOMENT OF YOUR TIME...?

GRRRRR'R

20

SHERLOCK HOLMES! ZE GREAT ENGLEESH DETECTIVE! OUI? I KNOW OF YOU FROM YOUR BOOKS, MONSIEUR! PLEASE, DO COME IN!

WE SHOULD APOLOGIZE, MADAME, FOR CALLING UNANNOUNCED...

I SEE NO REASON FOR PLEASANTRIES, WATSON.

MADAME--I ACCUSE YOU OF AIDING AND GRANTING REFUGE TO THE KILLER COUNT DRACULA! IT'S NO GOOD TO DENY IT-- I KNOW YOU WERE AT CARFAX ABBEY IN HIS BEHALF...I KNOW YOU HAVE BEEN PROTECTING HIM!

PARDON?? I DON'T... UNDERSTAND. CARFAX? DRACULA?

SHE WILL LIE, OF COURSE.

AND THEY WILL BELIEVE ...ALREADY WATSON'S FACE HAS SOFTENED TO HER.

WHY AM I THE ONLY ONE TO SEE THROUGH THE PAINT AND PERFUME?

NEVER... HAVE I HEARD OF SUCH THINGS.

I THINK-- PERHAPS--YOU HAVE!

THERE-- WATSON! THERE! DO YOU SEE? THE WOUNDS IN THE THROAT!

GOOD LORD--MONSTROUS! MADAME BERNHARDT...YOU MUST TRY TO BELIEVE WE ARE TRYING TO HELP--

LET ME LOOSE! I WILL NOT BE MANHANDLED!

GRROOWWLL

WOMEN ARE NATURALLY SECRETIVE, WATSON, AND THEY DO THEIR OWN SECRETING VERY WELL...

...WHERE BETTER TO HIDE SOMETHING--THAN IN THE OPEN?

WHO ELSE BUT WE WOULD FIND A PROP COFFIN CONTAINING A SPRINKLE OF DIRT-OMINOUS?

THE TRUTH--MADAME BERNHARDT! YOU MUST TELL US, FOR THAT IS YOUR ONLY SALVATION.

WHAT'S GOING ON HERE?

I'D BE LEAVING IF I WERE YOU, GENTLEMEN-- IF YOU TAKE MY MEANING.

21

I SHOULD NOT HAVE HAVE REMAINED AFTER *SUNDOWN*.

I SHOULD NOT HAVE LEFT AMSTERDAM.

NO.

THAT ISN'T TRUE.

I AM *NEEDED* HERE...

...THEY...

...NEED...

...ME...

THUNK

FOOLISH.

STUPID.

OLD MAN.

TOO SLOW. TOO TIRED.

I CAN NOT DIE.

GOTT...

NOT NOW.

NOT WITH ALL THESE LIVES ON MY *CONSCIENCE*...

...ALL THIS *BLOOD* ON MY HANDS...

SINGULARITY IS INVARIABLY A CLUE, WATSON... THE THEATRE POSTER-- COUPLED WITH THE ODD QUOTE FROM VAN HELSING'S BEGGAR WOMAN, THE EVIDENCE OF GREASE-PAINT... THE CONNECTION TO SARAH BERNHARDT OBVIOUSLY PRESENTED ITSELF.

IT ALWAYS SEEMS SIMPLE AFTER YOU *EXPLAIN* IT. HOLMES--

--HOW DEEPLY INVOLVED IS SHE IN ALL THIS?

A WOMAN'S HEART AND MIND ARE INSOLUABLE PUZZLES TO THE MALE, OLD FRIEND-- REGARDLESS HOW ADMIRABLE SHE MAY APPEAR.

AH! MR. HOLMES-- YOU'VE A VISITOR, SIR. A CLIENT, I THINK. A MOST RE-FINED GENTLE-MAN.

23

1

WITH YOUR CROSSES AND YOUR WAFERS...

WE ARE THE MASTERS OF THIS CITY...

IN... GOTT'S NAME--

--NO!

FOOL...

RRROOOARRR

BACK... BACK!

②

GOTT *HELP* ME.

RRROOARR

AAIIEEEE

INSPECTOR *LESTRADE!* OVER THERE! *LOOK!*

I TOUCHED *NOTHING,* SIR. SHE WAS JUST LIKE THIS WHEN I FOUND HER.

YOU DID *PROPERLY* IN ASKING FOR ME, STEVENSON. I'M SURE THIS *MURDER* IS CONNECTED WITH THE OTHERS...

...ONLY WHY SO FAR FROM WHITE-CHAPEL AND *WHERE* IS ALL THE *BLOOD?*

SIR--COULD THIS BE OUR MAN?

I'M AFRAID NOT, BLAKELY. I THINK I *KNOW* HIM... *DOCTOR VAN HELSING--?*

JA... JA...

I *THOUGHT* AS MUCH. A BIT OF A KOOK... HELPED GREGSON ONCE ON A CASE INVOLVING WITCH-CRAFT.

EASY THERE, BLAKELY! HE'S BADLY HURT. STEVENSON--GET HIM TO THE HOSPITAL.

NO... NO HOSPITAL... TAKE ME... TAKE ME TO SHERLOCK HOLMES.

3

YOU MUST HAVE NO MISUNDER-STANDINGS, HOWEVER...MY MOTIVES IN THIS ARE **RE-VENGE** AND PERSONAL JUSTICE. I CARE LITTLE FOR THIS CITY, OR THE PEOPLE IN IT.

I WANT THE WOMAN-- **LUCY.** ONCE I HAVE HER YOU MUST NOT INTERFERE.

I CAN ASSURE YOU OF **NOTHING** AT THIS STAGE. BE PREPARED TO SEEK SHELTER THIRTY MINUTES BEFORE DAWN AS I'VE DIRECTED. WE WILL MEET YOU IN THE PREARRANG-ED PLACE.

I MUST **INSIST**, MR. HOLMES.

TAKE YOUR FILTHY--

AKKK!

WATSON!

YOU CAN NOT PLAY YOUR BRAINS AGAINST **MINE**, DETEC-TIVE.

I WILL CLEAVE THE WAY TO **MORIARTY**...

...BUT THE **WOMAN** IS **MINE.**

UNTIL **TONIGHT**-- GENTLE-MEN...

NEVER FELT... SUCH **STRENGTH**...

EASY NOW-- LET ME GET YOU A BRANDY.

KNOK KNOK

COME IN-- BILLY!

⑤

WIGGINS AND THE IRREGULARS ARE HERE, SIR.

ARE... YOU *CERTAIN* THIS PLAN WILL WORK, HOLMES?

NOTHING'S *ABSOLUTE*, OLD FELLOW.

BUT-- WITH LUCK, AND *KNOWLEDGE*, ON OUR SIDE... WE WILL END THIS 'VAMPIRE' PLAGUE *TONIGHT*.

SEND THEM UP, BILLY.

6

GET OUT. I LEFT ORDERS NOT TO BE *DISTURBED.*

I'M *SORRY,* PROFESSOR.

IT'S ABOUT *SHERLOCK HOLMES...*

I WILL RETURN, ANNA. DO NOT FEAR...NOTHING SHOULD HAPPEN FOR ANOTHER 24 HOURS.

I UNDERSTAND, PROFESSOR.

WHAT OF *HOLMES?*

I HAVE CONTINUED MY *VIGIL* IN BAKER STREET AND...HOLMES HAS APPARENTLY *RECOVERED.* BOTH HE AND...THE *COUNT* ARE PLANNING TO STRIKE AGAINST YOU!

DRACULA! ALIVE?

WHAT ARE THEY PLANNING? *TELL ME!*

I--I DON'T KNOW...I WAS... *STARTLED* BY THE COUNT'S APPEARANCE... I RUSHED BACK HERE--

IDIOT! MORAN! COME HERE!

PROFESSOR--?

YOU ARE TO TAKE FIFTY MEN TONIGHT AND CORNER OFF BAKER STREET COMPLETELY. I PLAN TO MAKE AN IMMEDIATE CALL. TAKE *MEN*-- YOU UNDERSTAND-- NOT CREATURES LIKE *THIS ONE.*

AND NOW... TIME FOR YOUR *REWARD...*

⑦

MRS. HUDSON WILL HAVE OUR HEADS FOR **STINKING** UP THE HOUSE WITH ALL THIS GARLIC--POOR OLD GIRL WILL NEVER KNOW THIS STUFF WILL SAVE HER **LIFE.**

INDEED, MY GRAVEST FEAR IS THAT SHE MAY SUDDENLY BELIEVE WE HAVE TURNED **RELIGIOUS,** AND WISH US TO JOIN HER AT CHURCH THIS SUNDAY.

TAKE CARE TO JAM UP THE KEY-HOLE TOO, WATSON.

" HOLMES...WHEN THAT HORRIBLE COUNT SPOKE OF REVENGE AGAINST LUCY WESTENRA--DO YOU BELIEVE HE AIMS TO **KILL** HER ? "

" IN LISTENING TO VAN HELSING, WE MAY BELIEVE SHE IS **ALREADY** DEAD."

"I SUPPOSE SO-- BUT THE **LOOK ON HIS FACE**...HOW COULD ANYONE TAKE SUCH PLEASURE AT THE THOUGHT OF COMMITTING **MURDER?**"

"IN THE WORLD OF COUNT DRACULA, I DON'T IMAGINE THERE ARE MANY **OTHER** PLEASURES, WATSON."

"**CHILLING** THOUGHT, HOLMES. I HOPE WIGGINS AND THE OTHERS ARE ALL RIGHT. "

"IF THEY OBEYED MY INSTRUCTIONS--AND THEY'VE NEVER FAILED TO -- THE IRREGULARS ARE THE **SAFEST** HUMANS IN LONDON TONIGHT.BUT I DO CONFESS SOME **CONCERN** IN USING THEM THIS WAY... THERE WAS NO ONE ELSE IN WHOM I COULD TRUST. SCOTLAND YARD IS TOO BULL-HEADED FOR SUCH QUICK ACTION."

YOU DID WHAT YOU HAD TO DO, HOLMES.ENGLAND IS **FORTUNATE** TO HAVE YOU ON HER SIDE.

AS I AM TO HAVE **YOU,** OLD FRIEND. AT TIMES I WONDER IF YOUR FAITH IN ME IS NOT MY **GREATEST** STRENGTH.

NOW TRY AND GET SOME REST. I'LL WAKE YOU WHEN THE TIME IS READY.

8

KRREEKK

HARDLY.

AHHH... *PROFESSOR MORIARTY.* I CONFESS-- I DIDN'T EXPECT *THIS.*

BILLY--? IS THAT YOU...?

INEVITABLE, SURELY. KEEP YOUR VOICE LOW... I AM NOT ALONE, AND WE WOULDN'T WANT TO DISTURB YOUR LANDLADY-- OR LITTLE BILLY AT SO LATE AN HOUR.

QUITE SO. CLOSE THE DOOR.

WELL-WELL...IT HAS BEEN A LONG TIME. YOU HAVE LESS *FRONTAL DEVELOPMENT* THAN I REMEMBERED...BUT WE *BOTH* HAVE CHANGED, EH?

VERY COMFORTABLY FIXED HERE, AREN'T YOU? AS I GET ON IN LIFE--

--THE *LITTLE COMFORTS* APPEAL TO ME MORE AND MORE.

INDEED. PRAY TAKE A CHAIR, PROFESSOR. I CAN SPARE YOU *FIVE MINUTES* IF YOU'VE ANYTHING TO SAY.

ALL I HAVE TO SAY HAS ALREADY CROSSED YOUR MIND.

THEN, POSSIBLY, MY ANSWER HAS CROSSED *YOURS.*

HMPH. I SEE BY THE OCCUPIED HAT RACK THAT I MUST MAKE A-NOTHER USE FOR THIS CHAIR--TO INSURE OUR *PRIVACY.*

THUMP

A JAMMED DOOR WOULD NOT CONFINE WATSON FOR LONG--

--AND, AS IT SEEMS, WE HAVE *LITTLE* TO DISCUSS.

⑨

THEN, YOU STILL STAND *AGAINST* ME?

ABSOLUTELY.

YOU'LL WISH YOU *HAD NOT*, MR. HOLMES--YOU REALLY WILL. THIS IS A *MIGHTY* ORGANIZATION OF WHICH EVEN *YOU* CAN HARDLY REALIZE ITS RESOURCES.

KEEP YOUR HANDS WHERE I CAN SEE THEM!

AH, YES. IT'S A *DANGEROUS* HABIT TO KEEP A LOADED FIREARM IN YOUR POCKET.

WITHDRAW *VERY SLOWLY*, PROFESSOR.

SLOW ENOUGH--?

MY-- BUT YOU HAVEN'T MUCH CHANGED. STILL THINK THE WHOLE WORLD IS AGAINST YOU, EH?

YOUR *TIME* IS UP, PROFESSOR.

PLEASE *INDULGE* ME A MOMENT-- FOR OLD TIME'S SAKE...

...ON THE 25th OF JANUARY YOU INCOMMODED ME. BY THE MIDDLE OF FEBRUARY I WAS SERIOUSLY *INCONVENIENCED* BY YOU...

...FORCED TO FLEE THE COUNTRY--FOR AWHILE. AND NOW--AT THE CLOSE OF APRIL--I BELIEVE I'M IN POSITIVE *DANGER* OF LOSING MY *LIBERTY*.

HAVE YOU A SUGGESTION TO MAKE?

YOU MUST *DROP IT*-- MR. HOLMES! STAND CLEAR OR BE *TRODDEN UNDERFOOT*!

I FULLY INTEND TO... AFTER *SUNRISE*. YOUR PLAGUE WILL DISAPPEAR FOREVER, AND SCOTLAND YARD WILL HAVE FULL EVIDENCE AGAINST YOU.

DON'T HOPE TO PUT ME ON THE *GALLOWS*... I ASSURE YOU *THAT* WILL NEVER HAPPEN.

I DON'T RELISH RE-OPENING THE *PAST*, MR. HOLMES--

--BUT, YOU RECALL, THEY'VE TRIED THAT BEFORE. YOUR BROTHER MYCROFT, *HE'S* THE ONE WHO SAVED ME, TOLD THE *TRUTH*...

...SOMETHING *YOU* COULDN'T DO. IT WAS *YOUR* MOTHER--NOT I-- WHO *POISONED* THE CHILD...

THAT'S ENOUGH!

...SHE WAS THE *MURDERER*, NOT I.

10

PITY ABOUT LITTLE SHERRINGFORD...THE HOLMES BROTHERS WERE ALL SO BRIGHT-- EAGER TO LEARN.

YES, I'M LEAV- ING-- BUT KNOW WELL IF I AM TO FALL, THIS TIME **WE WILL GO DOWN TO- GETHER.**

I PROMISE YOU.

A WICKED MAN...

...AN **EVIL** MAN.

AND I...

...I AM RESPONSIBLE.

DAMN ME TO HELL.

MORIARTY...THE ECCENTRIC TUTOR... THE **OBVIOUS** SUSPECT.

THE MERE SUSPICION COST HIM HIS CAREER...EMBITTER- ED HIM, **DARKENED** HIM.

HOW...HOW COULD I HAVE CONFESSED MY OWN MOTHER...WAS **THE MONSTER**--?

HOLMES! HOLMES!

THUD THUD THUD

OPEN THE DOOR!

...SO, YOU SEE, I COULDN'T JUST **TAKE HIM** -- NOT NOW, WITH SUCH NEEDLESS RISK TO MRS. HUDSON AND BILLY. NOT TO MENTION **YOU**, OLD FRIEND.

I UNDER- STAND, OF COURSE...I SUPPOSE I PANICKED WHEN I COULDN'T GET OUT. I SENSED MORIARTY WAS HERE.

YOU ARE DEVELOP- ING THE TRUE **INSTINCTS** OF A DETECTIVE, WATSON-- BUT I BELIEVE IT WOULD BE BEST IF YOU WERE TO LEAVE THE CITY AFTER DAWN.

UNTIL MORIARTY IS CAPTURED, I'LL BE A **DANGEROUS** COMPANION.

DON'T BE RIDICULOUS, HOLMES. I'LL SEE THIS THROUGH.

THANK YOU, MY FRIEND. YOUR TRUST IS ADMIRABLE.

"I ONLY PRAY OUR FAITH IN **DRACULA** IS JUSTIFIED."

"...AND YOU REALLY EXPECT ME TO *BE-LIEVE* ALL THIS ROT--?

"WILD TALES OF *GHOSTS* AND *MONSTERS* HAUNTING THE STREETS...

"...CHANGING PEOPLE INTO WALKING *CORPSES!*

"HOW COULD IT BE POSSIBLE?

"THIS IS 19th CENTURY LONDON...

"...NOT THE DARK AGES.

"WE'VE ENOUGH *MURDERERS, THIEVES* AND *RAPISTS* TO KEEP US BUSY AT THE YARD...

"...WITHOUT ADDING SPOOKS AND HOBGOB-LINS!

"I ASK FOR *PROOF,* MR. HOLMES--

"-- WHERE IS YOUR EVIDENCE?"

13

GRROWLL

MY GOD.

DO NOT FEAR, HERR HOLMES-- A VAMPIRE CAN NOT ENTER A DWELLING WITHOUT FIRST BEING *INVITED* BY SOMEONE INSIDE!

GRRRR

EXACTLY, DR. VAN HELSING.

AT ANY RATE--

"--IT IS *TOO LATE.*"

BONG

"6 O'CLOCK, PRECISELY."

BONG

BONG BONG

"I DON'T UNDERSTAND, MR. HOLMES... A HALF-HOUR BEFORE DAWN--ON A FRIDAY-- AND THE *CHURCH BELLS* ARE RINGING?"

BONG BONG

"LIVE AND LEARN, LESTRADE."

"BUT I STILL DON'T--"

"I BELIEVE I COMPREHEND YOUR PLAN, HERR HOLMES."

"YOU SHOULD PARTICULARLY APPRECIATE THIS, DR. VAN HELSING."

BONG BONG

HOLMES, AGAIN.

ALWAYS HOLMES.

BONG

TO THE END.

15

BONG

BONG

I STILL DON'T GET IT.

A **BRILLIANT** STRATEGY, HERR HOLMES.

ABSOLUTELY, MY FRIEND.

"IT IS SIMPLICITY ITSELF, LESTRADE--"

"YOU SEE, INSPECTOR-- OH... MAY I, HOLMES?"

"BY ALL MEANS, WATSON. YOU KNOW MY METHODS."

"THANK YOU. THE **IRREGULARS** ARE RINGING THE BELLS--ALL ACROSS LONDON,...

BONG

"...AND THEY HAVE BEEN ORDERED BY HOLMES TO KEEP RINGING--

"UNTIL THE **SUN** COMES UP."

"SOUNDS LIKE SOME KIND OF **PRANK**."

BONG

"COME-COME, LESTRADE...

"...MUST WATSON **SPELL IT OUT** TO YOU?"

"THOSE ARE **STEEPLE BELLS** RINGING, HERR INSPECTOR-- FROM **SANCTIFIED GROUND**--

"--TO VAMPIRES THE SOUND OF THEM IS THE VERY **CLAMOR OF HEAVEN**...

"...AFFECTING OUR FOES WITH **PARALYSIS** -- MAKING IT IMPOSSIBLE FOR THE MONSTERS TO SEEK THEIR RESTING PLACES.

"AND NOW AS THE SUN RISES--

"-- THEY CAN NOT ESCAPE."

16

THE SOLUTION IS -- AS YOU WOULD SAY-- *ELEMENTARY*.

YOU MEAN IT'S ALL OVER? *JUST LIKE THAT...?!*

THE UNDEAD OF LONDON ARE *DESTROYED* WITH THE SWEEP OF A SECOND HAND! I WONDER...HAS DRACULA ALSO FALLEN?

IF HE HAS SURVIVED, I DOUBT HE'LL REMAIN IN LONDON FOR LONG.

JA, NOT AFTER THIS. HE WOULDN'T *DARE!*

IT HAS BEEN AN HONOUR AND PRIVILEGE TO OBSERVE YOUR METHODS, HERR HOLMES.

LIKEWISE, DR. VAN HELSING.

I HOPE WE MEET AGAIN.

DEATH. *TRUE DEATH.*

THE SMELL OF IT IS EVERYWHERE.

WORSE THAN I EVER WOULD HAVE IMAGINED.

NONE EVEN MANAGED TO SEEK THE LOWER CHAMBERS--

--AWAY FROM THE LIGHT.

THE PITCH-SMEARED WINDOWS ARE ALL BROKEN...WALL PLANKS--*SHATTERED.*

TO LET IN THE SUN.

IT IS *DRACULA'S* DOING.

PROFESSOR! OH DEAR GOD--IT WAS HORRIBLE! *HORRIBLE!* THE SCREAMING...THE HOWLING... *THE BELLS.*

CALM YOURSELF, ANNA. IT IS OVER.

GO AND PACK OUR BAGS-- WE ARE NOT STAYING HERE AFTER DUSK. WE SHALL AWAIT AGATHA'S RISING...AND THEN LEAVE THIS WRETCHED CITY FOREVER.

TONIGHT.

17

"YOU." "YOU LEAD THEM HERE..."

...LUCY!

DISOBEDIENCE! CARELESSNESS! YOUR FOOLISH PRIDE HAS *RUINED* ME!

I DO NOT LIKE YOUR TONE, PRO-FESSOR.

I WARNED YOU TO STAY TO THE LOWER CHAMBERS-- BUT YOU FLAUNTED YOURSELF BEFORE DRACULA, MAKING HIM MY ENEMY.

DRACULA WOULDN'T HAVE TRUSTED YOU FOREVER.

YOUR *STUPIDITY* IS BURNED INTO YOUR FACE! ALL THAT'S MATTERED TO YOU IS YOUR ANIMAL LUST--!

HAVE YOU FORGOTTEN I SAVED AGATHA FROM *DEATH?*

BITCH! YOU PRO-FANE HER WITH YOUR FILTHY LIPS! I WISH I'D *STOPPED* YOU! I WISH--

YOUR *REGRETS* MEAN NOTHING TO ME! DON'T YOU REALIZE-- EVEN NOW-- *WHAT I AM?!*

SILLY LITTLE MAN.

DON'T YOU KNOW ANY-THING...?

EEEEEEE EE

18

19

"I FEEL LIKE WE'RE **RUNNING**, HOLMES -- RUSHING OFF TO SWITZERLAND LIKE FUGITIVES."

"I TEND TO AGREE, WATSON, BUT -- FOR ONCE -- I BELIEVE LESTRADE MAY BE CORRECT..."

...OUR STAYING IN LONDON WOULD ONLY HAMPER THE POLICE DURING THE ARRESTS. I PROVIDED THE EVIDENCE AGAINST MORIARTY -- NOW THE **LAW** MUST TAKE ITS COURSE.

BUT SURELY WE'D STILL BE A GREAT HELP IN CLEARING UP THESE MYSTERIES!

WE ARE NOT RETAINED BY SCOTLAND YARD TO DISPLAY THEIR **DEFICIENCIES**.

BESIDES, WE'RE NOT TURNING OUR BACKS ON LONDON, OLD FELLOW -- RATHER WE MAY WELL BE **SAVING** IT.

"YOU'RE WORRIED ABOUT MORIARTY'S **THREATS**. I COULD FEEL SOMETHING WAS DISTURBING YOU."

"NOT FEAR FOR MYSELF, WATSON, BUT FOR THE CITY. IN DESTROYING MORIARTY'S ORGANIZATION I FEEL **COMPLETED**. MY CAREER HAS REACHED ITS SUMMIT."

"I ONLY PRAY MY ABSENCE WILL FREE LONDON FROM HIS **BULLS-EYE**."

"AND WHAT OF THE **COUNT'S** DISAPPEARANCE, HOLMES? WE PRACTICALLY LET HIM ESCAPE."

"THAT WAS... UNFORTUNATE. I SHUDDER TO THINK OF WHERE HE IS HEADED."

TO BE CLAIMED BY COUNT DRACULA LONDON ENGLAND.

"AT LEAST HE IS DONE WITH US."

WE'RE NOT EVEN SETTLED IN AND YOU'RE ALREADY GETTING MESSAGES?

HMMM. AH, NO -- SEEMS YOUR REPUTATION HAS EXCEEDED US THIS TIME, DOCTOR.

WHAT DO YOU MEAN?

IT'S FROM THE HOTEL MANAGER. SEEMS AN ENGLISH WOMAN HAS COLLAPSED FROM FEVER AND IS BEGGING FOR AN ENGLISH DOCTOR. HE BEGS YOU TO COME -- HE FEARS SHE MAY BE DYING.

GOOD GOD!

WHY, OF COURSE, I **MUST** GO! THIS COULD TAKE QUITE A WHILE, HOLMES --

I UNDERSTAND. DO WHAT YOU MUST.

REICHENBACH, BETWEEN US. IF WATSON IS THERE -- YOU KNOW. ONE HOUR. MORIARTY.

WE'LL SEE THE SIGHTS TOMORROW, HOLMES. ADIEU FOR THE MOMENT.

ADIEU... MY DEAR WATSON.

22

HOLMES...

IT IS SUNSET AND I AM COMING FOR YOU... HOLMES...

SHERLOCK HOLMES IS GONE, MORIARTY.

HOWEVER...

I REMAIN.

DRACULA--?

DID YOU THINK I COULD FORGET?

YOUR DECEPTION. YOUR BE-TRAYAL. YOUR CORRUPTION OF LUCY.

MY LUCY.

NOW YOU'VE BAS-TARDIZED MY BLOOD--INJECTING YOURSELF TO ASSURE VICTORY AGAINST THE DETECTIVE. THE ULTIMATE BLASPHEMY.

I AM THE KING OF MY KIND.

MORIARTY...

...YOU ARE NOTHING.

SNAP

NO!

REVENGE! I HAVE THE RIGHT!

26

FOR LUCY.

...I JUST DON'T SEE WHY YOU CAN'T RETURN WITH ME.

I'VE EXPLAINED THAT, WATSON. MORIARTY MAY WELL HAVE BEEN BEHIND HALF THE EVIL IN LONDON, BUT HE WASN'T THE ONLY MAN WHO SWORE MY DEATH--LESTRADE'S TELEGRAM STATED THREE SUCCESSORS ESCAPED ARREST, FLEEING INTO EUROPE.

THEIR HATRED OF ME WILL INCREASE UPON NEWS OF THEIR MENTOR'S DEATH AT MY HANDS.

IT'S UP TO YOU TO CONVINCE THE WORLD OF MY OWN DEMISE IN YOUR PUBLISHED ACCOUNT OF THE CASE. THEN, THE MINIONS WILL LAY THEMSELVES OPEN FOR DESTRUCTION.

I DREAD TO THINK OF THE PUBLIC OUTCRY AT THE NEWS OF YOUR 'DEATH', HOLMES...BUT YOU MAY COUNT ON ME.

I WILL MISS YOU.

YOU'RE STILL WEARING THAT CRUCIFIX, HOLMES. A SOUVENIR, PERHAPS?

HMM? OH, YES. THE CROSS. CURIOUS. I'D FORGOTTEN ABOUT IT.

THIS WAS A GIFT, WATSON--A VERY LONG TIME AGO. FROM MY... MOTHER.

YOUR MOTHER! I ALWAYS ASSUMED YOU AND YOUR BROTHER WERE ORPHANS, HOLMES. YOUR MOTHER... LITTLE DID SHE KNOW THAT ONE DAY THAT KEEPSAKE WOULD SAVE YOUR LIFE. HOW IRONIC!

YES, MY DEAR WATSON...

"...HOW IRONIC, INDEED."

27

EPILOGUE II

MY REVENGE IS DONE.

I SHALL NOT RETURN TO THE RUSH AND FLOW OF LONDON. THERE ALL THAT REMAINS FOR ME IS DEATH...AND BITTER MEMORIES.

AND VAN HELSING.

HE WILL HOUND ME.

EVENTUALLY FIND ME...

OH! PLEASE EXCUSE ME, SIR.

I STEPPED OUT FOR SOME AIR--I DIDN'T KNOW THE PLATFORM WAS OCCUPIED.

NO NEED TO APOLOGIZE. YOU DID NOT DISTURB ME.

YOU'RE JUST BEING KIND. I'LL LEAVE YOU TO YOUR PRIVACY--

NO-- WAIT! PLEASE...

PLEASE STAY. JUST TALK TO ME AWHILE.

I... BUT--OF COURSE.

OF COURSE, I'LL STAY--IF YOU WANT ME TO.

IT'S A TERRIBLE THING TO TRAVEL ALONE, DON'T YOU THINK?

WE'RE NOT ALONE NOW

EVEN IF IT'S JUST FOR THE MO- MENT...

...WE CAN HAVE EACH OTHER.

FOR MARTHA.

END

28

Sherlock Holmes

Count Dracula

SCARLET IN GASLIGHT Sketchbook

Professor Moriarty

Van Helsing

Dr. Watson

Lucy Westenra

SCARLET IN GASLIGHT Sketchbook

Miscellaneous sketches

SCARLET IN GASLIGHT Sketchbook

A pencilled page by artist Seppo Makinen from Chapter Two.

AFTERWORD

On our earlier collaborations Martin Powell never mentioned being a Sherlock Holmes fan.

I had only read a couple of books on the subject.

When he suggested doing *Scarlet In Gaslight* I was not 100% sure I wanted to do this.

With some additional reading, photocopied references from Martin plus a few trips to the Metropolitan Toronto Library's Conan Doyle collection room, I felt ready to tackle this.

Now I hope that the critics will continue to be kind to us and Eternity Publishing will find our next case worth printing as a graphic novel too.

The game is a foot, but I find it not be elementary.

Seppo Makinen
June 1988

**His Mighty London Has Gone Mad.
Watson Has Abandoned Him.
And He Must Face An Enemy Who Can Not Be Seen.**

Strange occurrences are plaguing
London. A fruit vendor sees an apple
hanging in mid-air like a balloon,
a petty thief claims to have seen a
ghostly apparition with internal
organs visible, and a large quantity
of obscure drugs have been stolen
from London chemists.

The World's Greatest Detective
is called on the scene by Scotland
Yard to uncover the mystery of this
so-called Invisible Man. This case
has no supernatural overtones:
the Invisible Man is a creature of
science, not magic. This makes it
a natural for Holmes' powers of
deduction.

A Case Of Blind Fear is
scheduled for February 1989 release.

Opposite: Illustration by Seppo Makinen for
A Case Of Blind Fear

PRIVATE EYES
The Saint returns.
#1-3 $2.50ea
#4 (60 pp) $3.50
#5 (60 pp) $3.50
#6 (60pp) $3.50

PUBLIC ENEMIES
Classic Crime
#1-2 $4.00 ea

RETIEF
Keith Laumer's
famous creation
stars in all new
adventures!
#1-3 $2.50ea

RIPPER
#1 $6.00
#2 $4.00
#3-6 $3.00ea

ROBIN HOOD
#1-3 $2.50ea

**ROBOTECH II:
THE SENTINELS**
#1 (1st printing)
$4.00
#1 (2nd printing)
#2-6,8-14 $2.50ea
Wedding Special
#1-2 $2.50ea
Full color poster
$6.95

**ROBOTECH II:
THE SENTINELS
The Malcontent
Uprisings**
#1-3 $2.50ea
Full color poster
$6.95

SCIMIDAR
Book I #1-2 $2.50ea
Book II #1 (first
printing) $6.00
Book II #1 (2nd
printing) $3.00
Book II #2 (2nd
printing) $3.00
Book II #3 $3.00
Book III #1 $6.00
Book III #2 $3.00

**SHATTERED
EARTH**
#2-4,5,7-9 $2.50ea

**SHERLOCK
HOLMES**
The classic '50s
comic strip
#2-10, 12-22
$3.00ea
Casebooks #1-2
$2.50ea

**SHERLOCK
HOLMES of '30s**
#1-4 $3.50ea

**SHURIKEN: COLD
STEEL**
#1 $1.50ea
#3-4, 6 $2.50ea

**SHURIKEN
TEAM-UP**
#1 $2.00

SINBAD
#1-4 $2.50ea

**SOLO
EX-MUTANTS**
#2-4,5-6 $2.50ea

SPICY TALES
#1,2, 4, 8,10-17
$3.00ea

STREET HEROES
#1-2 $2.50ea

TEAM: NIPPON
#1-7 $2.50ea

**THREE
MUSKETEERS**
#1-3 $2.50ea

TIGER-X
Original series
#1, 3 $2.50ea
Book II #1-4 $2.50ea

TOM CORBETT
#1-3 $2.50ea

**TORRID
AFFAIRS**
'50s romance.
#1-2 $2.50ea
#3-5 (60 pp) $3.50ea

**TOUGH GUYS &
WILD WOMEN**
#1-2 $3.00 ea

**TROUBLE
WITH GIRLS**
Volume 1: #?, 9,
11-14 $2.50ea
Annual #1 $3.50
V2 #5, 7-9, 11-14
$2.50ea

**TWILIGHT
AVENGER**
#1,3, 5-6, 8 $2.50ea

VAMPYRES
#1, 3-4 $2.50ea

VERDICT
#1,3-4 $1.00ea

VICTIMS
#1-5 $2.50ea

VIDEO CLASSICS
Mighty Mouse!
#1-2 (60pp) $3.50ea

WALKING DEAD
All new Zombie
Horror by Jim
Somerville
#1-4 $2.50ea

WARLOCK 5
#16-22 $2.50ea
Book II #1-7 $2.50ea

WARLOCKS
#1 $3.00
#2-10 $2.50ea

**WAR OF THE
WORLDS**
#1-3, 5 $2.50ea

**WEREWOLF AT
LARGE**
#3 $2.50ea

WILD KNIGHTS
#1 $3.00
#2-10 $2.50ea

• GRAPHIC NOVELS •

ABBOTT & COSTELLO
The crazy comedy duo is back in this classic collection of the misadventures from the '40s and '50s.

CHINA SEA
An epic adventure in the tradition of Terry and the Pirates.

DINOSAURS FOR HIRE
Three gun-crazy Dinosaurs on the loose as private eyes!

FU MANCHU
Sax Rohmer's villainous creation stars in two classic adventures.

NINJA HIGH SCHOOL
One boy, two girls, giant robots. Trouble ahead.

PERRY MASON
The world's most famous lawyer stars in four classic cases.

PLAN 9 FROM OUTER SPACE
The only authorized adaptation of the worst movie ever made!

PLAN 9 FROM OUTER SPACE
The original, uncensored, illustrated screenplay by Edward D. Wood, Jr.!

SCARLET IN GASLIGHT
An all new epic adventure pitting the world's greatest detective against Cound Dracula!

SCIMIDAR
The adventures of a female bounty hunter in the year 2005.
Contains nudity and sexual situations.

SHERLOCK HOLMES
The world's greatest detective is featured in 6 full length adventures from the newspaper strip of the '50s.

SPICY DETECTIVE STORIES
Illustrated fiction from the naughty pulps of the '30s and '40s.

SPICY TALES
Uncensored comics from the pulps of the '30s.

TEEN ANGST
A treasury of pre-code '50s romance stories.

THREE STOOGES
Nyuk! Nyuk! Nyuk! The Knuckleheads return in collection of their looney antics.

THREE MUSKETEERS
All for one and one for all in this new adaptation of the classic Dumas novel.

TIGER-X
In the late 20th Century, a Soviet invasion has split the U.S. in two.

TROUBLE WITH GIRLS
Lester Girls longs for the quiet life, if only the fabulous babes, ninja assassins, and relentless reporter Maxi Scoops could leave him alone.

WAR OF THE WORLDS
The Aliens Have Landed! Based on the H.G. Wells novel.